T0113931

Once Upon a Time in Alabama …

On One Very Magic Christmas Eve

Sonya Lyatsky

WESTBOW
PRESS®
A DIVISION OF THOMAS NELSON
& ZONDERVAN

WestBow Press books may be ordered through booksellers or by contacting:

WestBow Press
A Division of Thomas Nelson & Zondervan
1663 Liberty Drive
Bloomington, IN 47403
www.westbowpress.com
844-714-3454

Editor: Annie Seaton
Cover Illustrator: Nastia Danilova

ISBN: 978-1-6642-5119-9 (sc)
ISBN: 978-1-6642-5118-2 (e)

Print information available on the last page.

WestBow Press rev. date: 11/24/2021

To my dear husband
and all the good people of Alabama

Chapter 1

———❊———

"*N*oel, Noel, the angels did say!*" the people in the line were singing. Always! Even in the middle of summer!

Noel counted the money and gave it with a receipt to the sweaty, dirty guy in the yellow hard hat; the man signed the paper and departed, happily pocketing the money. The next construction guy, partially covered with white and blue paint, appeared in her trailer-office window.

"I am your snowman! Do you like your Santa, baby?" he said.

Someone in the line behind him shouted in response: "No way! He is too old for her."

"Baby," the man asked without paying attention to the shouts. "Can you ask Santa to fill my stocking?"

"Your stocking?" Guys in the line were horrified. "It stinks like a chemical weapon. You wanna kill our sweet little darling?"

So it goes. She had listened to endless Santa jokes for the six months she worked there. All this was happening because her father hadn't wanted to give her a simple and boring girl's name. He'd named her Noel! Yes, she was born on Christmas Eve, but so what? Should it be eternal Christmas?

"Hi Noel, say thanks to Santa!" said the next guy picking up his pay. "Can you give me more? I was a good boy!"

When the line ended, she closed the trailer window and inhaled deeply. Mr. Michael, Martha and Jill usually departed by that time, and the tiny office became very comfortable and quiet. It was time to relax. Soon it would be time for the long and boring calculations and filling out forms, but these ten minutes of total peace and solitude were her blessed moments ... but not today.

Today Mr. Michael had installed a television in the office, and when Noel fixed herself some tea, she almost unconsciously pushed the magic button. The two most handsome dark faces in the world appeared on the screen.

Oh, no! She loved this show! And it was the best episode of the previous season. The best episode ever. Brian Morgan played a therapist and Michael Jason played a patient. She had a crush on both of them, although Morgan was old enough to be more of a father figure for her. She'd made up so many dialogs with him in her mind. No, they were more monologs. Michael Jason, slick and stylish, was the man of her dreams. She had a poster of them over her table. No, she could not skip the show. But everything she worked on during commercial breaks had to be recalculated.

When at last she finished clicking the keys, saved and printed the file, it was almost eleven p.m. She wanted to swear. It was dangerous to walk home. The night was warm, so some drunk guys could be looking for trouble.

Noel wrapped herself in a baggy hoodie, found the pepper spray in her purse and clamped it in her fist. Then she locked the trailer, regretting that she'd wore flip-flops. Not the best choice if she needed to run fast.

Her trailer was located at the construction site. Several residential trailers were located outside the site along the street. The comfort of these wagons was nonexistent, but the price was low. The windows were dark; people were either already asleep or visiting local bars.

At first, the street looked empty, but then Noel noticed a man sitting on a bench at the bus stop.

"Well, it begins," she thought. "I hope he is too drunk to run after me."

The man with messy twists of black hair and a bandana on his forehead, wore jeans and T-shirt. He was sitting with his back to her and examining something in his hands. A bottle? No, it did not look like it. A cellphone?

In that moment, he raised his head and looked at something on the street. His dark red bandana sparkled in the streetlight, and Noel suddenly remembered him, his messy twists of black hair, unshaven jaw protruding forward, and a huge purple swelling birthmark all over his face. The mole was spreading through his cheeks, nose, and one of the eyelids, half closing his right eye. Probably on his forehead too but that was always covered by his bandana. Because of this swelling, the man looked really creepy. He lived in one of the trailers; he never smiled, usually stood in the line with a stony face, took his money and silently left. When she saw his face in her office window for the very first time, Noel had almost jumped and shrieked. What's his name? Nick? Rick? And suddenly she remembered: people call him Mickey Monster or Mickey Mutant. He didn't care. So, his name is Mickey…

Noel walked cautiously, hoping to slip by unnoticed. But suddenly she saw what he was holding; she could not believe her eyes: it was a book! The man who looked like a mutant-gangster was reading. Late at night, not with weed or a bottle, but with a book. It was amazing. In her mind, this book suddenly extracted him from the circle of dangerous people, and she took a step toward him, not understanding why.

"Er … Mickey? Hi?" she said softly. "How are you doing?"

Surprised, he turned to her, and for a while did not know what to say. It was evident that he was not ready to see any talking creatures emerge from a construction zone around midnight. Then he mumbled, "Yeah, hi."

"No buses at night," Noel said hesitantly.

"I know."

"Ah … well …" She paused, not knowing what else to say, but her curiosity took over. "Then what are you doing here?"

He shrugged and did not answer. It was obvious he did not want to talk. This calmed her even more, as well as the fact that he did not look drunk. He looked gloomy, but sober. So she made an attempt to smile.

"It's late, but it seems you work the first shift, so why are you not asleep?"

He turned away, paused, and then responded reluctantly, nodding toward the housing trailers.

"My roommate has a visitor. I'm waiting for them to finish." He spoke with a strong street accent; his speech was slurred, and his voice was low and muffled.

"Got it!" She smiled. "And how much longer do you have to wait?"

"Don't know. Maybe half an hour."

He looked at the book again. It was a cheap edition with a soft tattered cover. Noel wanted to read the name of the author, but instead, she noticed a library sticker on the book cover. This surprised her even more. The construction guy attending a library?

"Good writer?" she asked.

"Eh … it's almost midnight, are you gonna discuss literature?" he said in a slightly tense and ironic tone.

"Oh, sorry," she said, feeling embarrassed. "I just wanted to ask you…" she hesitated, "to accompany me if you have some spare time. It's dangerous; I stayed late. Needed to finish my work." She swallowed and added, "Don't think anything, I'm really afraid to walk alone.

Three days ago, a man was assaulted near our house, and a month ago, even worse, a girl…"

He glanced at her thoughtfully, then took an old denim jacket from the bench, stood up, and said in a calm and gentle voice:

"Let's go. How far?"

"Twenty minutes' walk. Well, maybe thirty … and why do you need a jacket? The night is so warm."

"For safety," he said. "Less likely that someone attacks. I don't like fighting," he added apologetically, and for the first time he smiled, barely noticeable. And his face changed—he had a gentle smile, but very sad.

Indeed, the baggy jacket made his figure look powerful. When he pushed his already protruding lower jaw forward he looked even dangerous. But Noel was already smiling at his trick, and she was not frightened anymore.

"Are you really not armed? What if someone attacks?"

"We'll run away together," he said, slightly smiling with the same sad smile.

"Well, if they attack, I'll protect you. I have pepper spray." Noel laughed, and now she felt at ease with joy in her heart. And she realized he was much younger than he'd seemed at first. "Not forty," she thought. "About thirty. Probably he looks older because he is unshaven."

His tactics worked. Sometimes, some shadowy figures appeared from the darkness but retreated back into the night without making problems. At first, they walked in silence. Noel felt somewhat awkward about it. She began to ask questions: where he came from, how old was he, etc.

Mickey responded briefly and reluctantly that he was from California, and he was thirty-two, had been on some religious study but did not finish. Then to avoid further inquiries, he started asking her questions.

She said that she was local, went to school a few miles away, worked at various diners. Now she was studying to be a nurse. She would like to be a doctor, but later. She told him that she worked two jobs to save money for college and her children. Her son, Derek, is four and daughter, Alisha, is three. She has a mother, Tressa, on disability and a sister, Leah, in high school. And feeling his sympathy and kindness, she opened further. No, she is not married. Got pregnant without thinking; she was deeply in love. Her high school boyfriend was trying to find a job in another state, then returned a year later with some money. They were going to get married and she got pregnant again. Then the boyfriend disappeared with the money. She never heard from him again.

"I have one more year of study," she said when they finally reached her house, resembling a hut under the trees on the dark street. "When I finish college, I will look for a job as a nurse; our life will be easier, could be..." and Noel spotted the dark silhouette of her mother in the brightly-lit window. She hesitated, not knowing what else to say, as her mother opened the door and appeared in the door frame, clutching her stick.

"Noel, it's almost midnight!" Tressa's voice was low and harsh. "And who is this?"

Despite her disability, she looked tough and determined.

Mickey took a step back, smiling uneasily and raising his hand as if saying, "hello."

"Mom," said Noel. "I asked Mickey to accompany me home. I needed to finish my work. And he lives and works on the construction site."

Mickey took another step back and his voice barely audible, he said, "Er ... goodnight." Then he turned around and started walking away fast. Noel didn't say anything, just stood and looked as he moved into the darkness. And suddenly she woke up and shouted after him, "Thank you!"

He didn't look back; he just lifted his right hand as if greeting someone at a distance.

"I almost don't even know him," Noel said apologetically in a muffled voice.

"That's exactly what I worry about," her mother answered glumly.

"Would it be better to walk alone?" Noel retorted a little angrily.

"Go inside," answered Tressa, unstuck from the doorframe, heavily stepping back with the support of her crutch.

Chapter 2

After that night, Noel caught herself involuntarily looking for the dark red bandana at the construction site. And sometimes she saw it high on the upper floors; Mickey wore it on his neck or covering his face; he had a hard hat on his head. Sometimes she saw him nearby, pushing a wheelbarrow or carrying a can of paint; she waved at him and he nodded passing by. Noel could not help smiling.

Sometimes she saw him without a shirt, wearing only dirty, torn jeans. She was surprised by the contrast of his face and body. He had an astonishingly beautiful, thin torso, a powerful chest, and prominent biceps. No tattoos visible; evidently, he had neither been in a youth gang nor in jail.

Soon she saw him when he came for his pay. That day, she was wearing a red dress, which collected comments and greedy looks from the whole line of men, but Mickey did not react. His name on the list was Michael Birch. He smiled a little, silently nodded in response to her greetings, waited his turn, signed a paper, and pocketed the money without counting. She asked what he was reading. He shrugged. "A book," and quietly disappeared.

Sometimes walking to work, she saw him on his morning run or doing pull-ups on local playgrounds, and in the evening, she could see him at the same bus stop with a book, but Martha occasionally gave her a lift, or Noel finished her work earlier and preferred to slip by unnoticed. It was not difficult since he was always sitting on the same bench facing the street and with his back toward her trailer-office.

❄ ❄ ❄

Sipping her tea on a short break after work and looking to the compassionate therapist's eyes on the poster, she mumbled, "Hi, Dr. Morgan, how are you doing?"

Of course, in the show, the name of the therapist was different, but she never could remember. And who really cares? And the actor Brian Morgan didn't object.

In her imagination, he answered, "Hello, Ms. Forest. I am fine, thank you for asking." Occasionally, he even called her Dr. Forest. Though sometimes he was not so formal and simply called her by her name. Then he usually added, "Tell me about your day."

"Well, let me think … my day … Today I get registered for the new semester; soon it will be real madness…"

"I know, you are very strong," answered Dr. Morgan. "You can do it". His voice was soft and kind, just like her father's voice.

"I am trying," answered Noel thoughtfully. "But sometimes I feel–" and her eyes slipped to the handsome face of Michael Jason.

"Never give up," said Michael with the same softness in his voice. "Don't you ever give up."

"Well, I am trying," whispered Noel.

Then in her imagination, Michael gave her flowers. White roses. And they were dancing. Oh, how gorgeous he was…

But then her thoughts drifted to reality and to the evening outside the trailer. And to the bench on a bus stop, where a lonely, ugly man was reading his book. And Noel wondered if he was deliberately sitting there?

She realized that she was thinking of him a bit more than she should.

Chapter 3

"Mommy, I want ice-cream!" said Derek.

"Well," said Noel, "Why not? Let's go."

It was Saturday, after lunch, and she'd just finished washing the fridge and cleaning the kitchen. The children were restlessly running around, Leah had disappeared with friends, and Tressa was having endless conversations on the phone.

Suddenly Noel thought, why don't we all go to the library? She looked for her card, but could not find it. It didn't stop her. She needed to update it anyway; she hadn't been there for a couple of years.

It was the usual hot end-of-summer day in Alabama. Noel slipped into her old, bright-blue dress, put Alisha and Derek into the double stroller, adjusted sunshades and navigated to the street. On the way through the sweet green town, they stopped to play at each playground, greet every pooch, and to make a break for ice cream.

When they finally reached the library, Alisha was already sound asleep in the stroller, and Derek landed in the children's section, pulling out a pile of books.

The library was quiet, cool, and almost empty; just some old ladies at the magazine tables and some high school students at the computers. Looking around, Noel suddenly realized that she was almost ready to see a dark red bandana. She shook her head at this thought.

She pushed the stroller with Alisha sleeping like an angel between the shelves, browsing the books, and from time to time, came back to check Derek. Everything was calm. Soon, Derek also fell asleep on the carpet floor, and Noel put him into the stroller, chattered with the elderly librarian lady, got a new card, checked out a bunch of books, stuffed them into the stroller bag and pushed the stroller to the exit.

One lady rose to open the door for her, but the door opened suddenly and Mickey entered the library holding a bag full of books. It was so unexpected that Noel stopped with her mouth open. He immediately grasped the situation and stepped back holding the door for her.

Noel said, "Hi, thanks," and could not say anything else. Miss Friendly! He also said, "Hi," and she passed by, pushing the stroller forward into the blazing sunlight, and quickly walked down the street to the shadows under the trees. She did not understand why she was in such a hurry.

When finally, she had the courage to look back, she saw that he stood there watching. She waved her hand, and he shouted softly in response, "Need help?"

She smiled, silently shook her head, and left without looking back again. And for some reason she felt he was still standing there, watching them until they turned around the corner.

Chapter 4

Some days later, during lunchtime, Martha took Noel to the grocery store as she often did. They didn't want to leave the food in the hot car so they unloaded everything into the fridge in the office. Martha promised to give her a ride after work, but she received a call from her home and drove off in a hurry.

When it was the time to go home, Noel opened the fridge and gave a deep sigh. And what was she gonna do now? At least she was wearing jeans, T-shirt, and sneakers, and not a red dress.

But the trip was going to be a torture. Maybe she could ask someone for help? Oh, yeah, no problem! But most of the guys would be making greasy jokes all the way. And afterward, they would behave like she owed them something. And they would know, where she lived. This was not good. Noel sighed again and start extracting her stuff from the fridge.

Loaded with bags and already figuring out how her palms would feel at the end of the trip, Noel locked the trailer and saw several workers who had just finished the shift, among them Freddy and Dean, local ladies' men.

Freddy instantly reacted with a greasy smile and open arms. "Noel, my beauty, I see you need help! I'm ready! I am always ready for such a beautiful girl!"

"Better let me help," fat Dean reacted, "or you'll never get rid of him!"

"Thanks, but no thanks. Please, mind your own business," said Noel slightly angrily. Yeah, it was exactly what she'd expected.

But suddenly she saw Mickey, who walked apart from the group. His hair, naked torso, and jeans were densely covered with whitish spray; sweat trickled down his shoulders. His bandana now looked more like a dirty rag. He noticed her, understood the situation instantly.

"Need help?"

She shrugged and smiled shyly. He nodded and said, pointing to her office: "Wait here, I'll be fast." She nodded happily and went back to the trailer.

He came clean in a gray T-shirt, sports pants, and wet bandana on his forehead. The water was still dripping from his messy hair twists. He also brought a large old backpack, placed it on the table in front of Noel and opened it.

"Put it all here."

She wanted to carry something herself, but he pointed to his bag without words. She obeyed. When the packing was completed, he put it on his back, and they left the trailer. The guys did not hesitate to comment, but Noel and Mickey both pretended not to hear.

At first, they walked in silence. She was afraid it would be difficult for him to carry such a load and talk at the same time, but he walked steadily; clearly, it was not hard for him.

Suddenly he asked her, "How are you? With kids? Is it hard to be alone?"

"At first it was hard," she said after a brief silence. "Then we got used to it. Mom helps, sometimes my sister, but she's very impulsive. A teenager."

"Yeah," he said, and the conversation died.

They walked for some time in silence again, and finally, she asked:

"What do you read? I mean … what do you like?"

He shrugged a little. "Detective stories, action..." he hesitated, then added embarrassed, "Poetry..."

"Poetry?" Noel was surprised. "What kind?"

He did not answer, regretting he had mentioned it at all. Instead, he asked, "And what do you read?"

"Well ..." She hesitated. "Basically textbooks. And with the kids, I don't have time for anything else. We don't even watch TV."

"Why?" he asked amused. "Everyone watches TV."

"It is broken," she said, smiling uncomfortably, and the conversation died again.

"Well, here we are," said Noel with relief when they reached their destination, and warily looked at her old house. The evening light was still good enough to see all the dried flowers and forgotten toys on the untrimmed lawn, the sagging gutters, the cracked window glass fixed with scotch tape, the peeled off paint. Noel felt piercing shame. At least she could water the flowers. And she froze inside as she opened the door, hoping not to see so much mess inside.

Mickey pretended not to notice.

When they entered, they heard the boy's wild shriek and equally wild girl's laughter. Alisha, screaming with delight, ran away from her brother, who was jumping after her with an inflatable alligator slightly bouncing her on the back with the toy. The moment they saw Noel, they rushed into her arms, happily screaming, "Mommy!" and unloading on her all the daily news.

Finally, the kids saw the stranger. Alisha hid herself in Noel's arms, but Derek put forward his toy and proudly said, "This is Roger! And who are you?"

"I am Mickey," said the guest smiling and asked Noel, "Where should I put the stuff?"

Noel rose, holding her daughter in her arms and smiling. "On the table, please." And she felt tremendous relief because the children were dressed clean and not smeared with anything.

Derek immediately noticed Mickey's birthmark.

"Did someone beat you up?" he asked with the innocence of a child.

"Derek!" exclaimed embarrassed Noel, but Mickey didn't hesitate.

"No," he said calmly to Derek and added for Noel. "It is okay."

"Does it hurt?" asked Derek again because he was unable to think about anything else.

"No, it doesn't," said Mickey, even more, calm and kind.

"It is ugly," said Derek. "Can I touch it?"

"No!" said Noel sharply.

"Who did it to you?" asked Derek again.

"A fairy," said Mickey, smiling with a sad smile. "She cast a spell, and I became ugly".

"Wow!" exclaimed Derek with a mixture of horror and delight. "A real fairy? Was she ugly?"

"No, she was not," answered Mickey. "She was quite beautiful."

That moment Tressa, in a green home dress and apron, appeared from the inner room with support of her crutch and stopped, observing the newcomer:

"Hello, how are you doing?"

"Hi, Mom," said Noel "This is Mickey. He helped me to bring home the groceries. Martha left earlier. She had some emergency at home."

"Well, thank you, Mickey. My name is Tressa." She sat heavily on the chair near the kitchen table and stretched out her hand.

Mickey made a step forward and took her palm, gently saying, "Hi." Then he turned to Noel and added, "Bye. See you."

"Oh, no!" exclaimed Noel, "We are going to eat first! I am so hungry! I bet you are too!" She added for Tressa, "He just finished the work shift."

"Er, I'm going to a diner," said Mickey.

"No, no, no," exclaimed Noel. "I am going to warm it up in five minutes. Come in! Go into the living room. Please…"

Mickey did not move, and it was clear that he wanted to leave. Noel lowered Alisha to the floor; the girl flew with a happy screech into the room, and Derek ran after her with the alligator. But a second later, Derek was back without the toy, but with a whole stack of children's books and ran straight toward Mickey.

"Look, what I have!"

"Oh!" The guest made a surprised and joyful face. "What is it?"

"Books," Derek exclaimed, while half of the books slipped to the floor from his hands.

"Oh. Books? Let's see." Mickey squatted down and picked up one of the books. "Look at this! What is it? Who is this monster?"

"It is an octopus!" Derek exclaimed, joyful that someone was interested. "You see, he has a head, and eight legs just out of his head!"

"Wow!" Mickey said astonished. "Where's his stomach?"

Derek puzzled, looked at the picture, then he touched his own tummy.

"There's no stomach," he said in surprise. "Only the head and legs. Mom, where is his stomach?"

"Probably in the head, since there's nothing else." Noel said, busy taking food from the fridge and preparing to warm it up. "Go to the room. Mom, please!"

Tressa took pity on her daughter, but she didn't want to leave the kitchen; she was too curious.

"Leah, can you please read to the kids?" she asked the girl in a yellow top and shorts, who appeared from the living room with a lollipop in her mouth.

"I can't," said Leah, "I am doing my homework." But she did not even make an attempt to leave, standing and looking at the guest with an appraising and skeptical stare.

"Mom?" said Noel with pleading in her voice.

"Yes, sure," answered Tressa, trying to get up.

"May I read to them?" Mickey asked suddenly, and everyone around froze in surprise.

"Er … okay," Noel said hesitantly.

Mickey sat on the floor near the pile of books, took one of them, and began reading aloud. Derek squatted down on his side, Alisha climbed up on her grandma's lap, and Leah stood nearby, all attention on the performance. This was something to listen to and see.

It was not just reading a book; it was a whole play. Mickey spoke with different cartoon voices. He growled like a giant and squeaked like a mouse, created voices of octopuses and monsters, piglets and a wolf; he showed them with his hands and face. It was an astonishing show. In a few minutes Derek was laughing out loud, and even Alisha climbed down and walked closer, watching the action, spellbound. And the astounded women did not even know what to say. Everyone felt relief when Noel finally said that dinner was ready. Although everyone was also feeling regret that such a wonderful performance ended.

They pulled out the table, which filled almost the entire small living room. Tressa sat at the head of the table; Mickey on the right, next to him sat Derek, not allowing anyone to take a place near his new champion. Noel with Alisha and Leah sat opposite the men's team. When everyone was seated, a plate of hot mashed potatoes, meatballs, and the deliciously smelling sauce were placed in front of everyone, and Derek was already reaching for the sauce with a spoon, but Tressa calmly stopped him. "Derek, you know that the prayer's first." Then she turned to the guest and said, "Do you want to say it?"

Mickey was surprised but did not object. Calmly and sincerely, he folded his hands and said "Our Father" as if he had done so many times. And he noticed that everyone, even Alisha, habitually folded their arms and bowed their heads, like this was a regular activity—not just a performance to impress a guest.

As the evening wore on, Noel was suddenly swept away by the inner sensation of a family: the family she imagined, what she saw in her dreams years ago, what she wanted to create. That dream had been lost, when she returned home from the hospital with her newborn baby girl. Dreams of such a family had ended for her she thought forever, but at that moment, suddenly came to life again so powerfully that she felt pain in her chest. And she wanted to live in this moment for a long, long time. She hoped that everyone was too busy to notice the tears in her eyes.

And when the mashed potatoes were finished, the tea was poured, and the bread with jam was distributed as dessert, Tressa began to ask the guest who he was, where he came from, and about his family. Mickey tried to limit the answers to what Noel already knew. But finally, her mother asked a question.

"Mickey, do you have children?"

He somehow shrank and blinked a few times. Then he inhaled convulsively and answered with a question. "Do I look like I have children?"

"Well, you know," Tressa said stubbornly and slowly, "in my opinion, you look exactly like a man who has children." She looked at him as if to challenge, like a woman who had been abandoned by a man and left to the mercy of fate, who raised children alone.

He understood her mood and her challenge and kept silent for a while. Then he lowered his eyes and answered with a dead voice. "Had. I had a baby."

From these few words, Noel's heart fell somewhere deep into her stomach. She was afraid to hear what was next.

"How? What happened?" quietly asked Tressa.

Mickey tilted his head even lower to the side, swallowed and quietly replied. "Accident."

"Oh my goodness …" said Tressa. "How? Why?"

Mickey made a deep sigh and whispered in a low voice. "Her mother was drinking and driving."

"Oh my goodness!" Tressa said even more quietly, laying her hand on her chest. "I'm so sorry."

There was a terrible silence at the table. Even Alisha and Derek sat quietly, although they did not understand what was going on. And Mickey also sat looking nowhere and seeing nothing; his palms on the table were trembling a little.

"How old was she?" Tressa asked quietly. She did not want to ask anything, but it was distressing to remain silent, not to ask anything, like to slam this suddenly opened door...

"Four," said Mickey as if waking up. He blinked, made a long and slow sigh through his suddenly moist nose, took out a wallet from his pocket and took out some photographs, extracting one, looked at it for a few seconds. Then he handed it to Tressa. "Lisa," he said. "Her name is Lisa ... was ..."

Tressa looked and gave it to Noel.

"What a wonderful angel," she said in a sad voice. In the photo was a beautiful dark-skinned girl with curly hair and huge sad eyes. "I'm sorry," Noel said, barely audible. Her throat tightened and she could not say anything else. And there was simply nothing more to say.

He nodded in return. Then he took out a bundle of bills held together with a rubber band from another pocket and put it on the table.

"Can I give it to you? I don't need it. I have everything, but you have needs. For children, for the house..."

"Mickey, no!" Tressa said surprised, "Don't! We are doing very well."

"Do you carry all the money with you?" asked Leah surprised.

"Well, I have to." He smiled sadly. "Dean, my roommate, is browsing through my stuff, pulling out a little. It's better for you than for him ... and ... thanks, it was very delicious. But I need to go," he said, addressing no one specifically. "Goodbye. Thank you."

He got up and suddenly went out of the house, leaving his bread and tea untouched.

Noel stood up, tried to follow him, but could not do it quickly because she had to push her daughter's highchair aside, and when she hurried out of the house, Mickey was nowhere to be seen. She called him but in vain.

She returned to the table and said after a silence, "I think we should return the money."

"Really?" Leah was disappointed. "But he said that's for the children!" and added, rationalizing, "if his roommate steals it anyway."

Noel and Tressa looked at each other not knowing what to say…

❄ ❄ ❄

Closing the children's book after reading it out loud five or six times, Noel was still sitting on a worn floor mat leaning against Alisha's bed, watching the kids peacefully sleep. Listening to the sounds of the old house, she could not stop thinking about everything that happened today and about Mickey and his little girl. And also she was thinking of Jimmy, her ex-boyfriend.

"You know, Dr. Morgan," she said in her imagination. "I wonder, does he ever think about Derek? Does he care a bit? Does he know that he has a daughter? Would he hesitate even a minute if, God forbid, something …"

She did not want to think further.

Chapter 5

The next day, Noel prepared lunch for Mickey, secretly from her mother, but could not find him. Instead, she fed the lunch to Martha, who didn't have time to make it. And the next day, she only saw Mickey somewhere high above on the construction but did not catch the moment of his departure. The next two days she had her classes.

Early evening, coming home from her college, Noel suddenly saw Mickey standing near her house on the folding ladder, fixing the rain gutters. Tressa was sitting nearby in the garden chair with Mr. Katz, the elderly neighbor. Kids were sitting on the neatly trimmed lawn laughing on something Mickey was telling them. This time Mickey refused to dine with them, to Derek's huge disappointment, and left before Noel finished cooking.

The next weekend, Mickey came with electric gear and inspected the entire house. He secured some loose outlets and replaced air filters, which no one had changed for years. And this time Derek didn't let him go until Mickey read some books; and he also shared their evening meal. It was peaceful and lovely …

"This is how it goes!" Martha was quietly giggling. "First, he is carrying your bags for you. Then you start feeding him. Then he fixes your outlets …"

She dived deeply into the ice-cream container with the large spoon, dropped the delicious white ball to her paper plate and pushed the container to Jill and Noel.

"Do you want some more?"

Noel thanked her and refused, but Jill took the ice-cream with pleasure.

"And do you know, what is the most dangerous part?" continued Martha, raising her spoon up. "You fantasize about him. You imagine how good and caring he is. You invent your future life together, and that's it. You are trapped! But not with a real person but with your own fantasies!"

"Oh, yeah," said Jill, with a mouth full of ice-cream. "With daydreams!"

"Don't trap yourself. Find someone with a position and money!" continued Martha.

"And good looking," said Jill, "You are so beautiful. And he is so ugly! Do you sleep with him?"

"No!" exclaimed Noel in frustration. "We are not sleeping together!"

"Find someone handsome," muttered Jill. "Jimmy was very handsome." She was Noel's classmate and remembered him well.

"Yes, he was," said Noel sadly. "And where is he now?"

"Well," murmured Jill skeptically. "What if it is your fault? Maybe you should do... something ... er ... to keep him?"

"What?" asked Noel. "What should I do? Exotic dancing? Japanese cuisine? Are you kidding? Do I need to please some irresponsible fool, who forgets his promises and his children? If you just make an attempt to please him, you'll never stop because he is never satisfied! If there is no love and respect, you cannot create it by pleasing!" she finished with disgust.

"Well, it is your life," said Martha.

"Mickey is kind," said Noel. "He has a heart. He's helpful and caring. Really. He's just hurt."

"She loved me for the dangers I had passed," Jill declared theatrically with a low voice like a man. "And I loved her that she did pity them."

"What is it?" asked Noel, after a short silence. "What selfish guy are you quoting?"

"Othello!" Jill exploded with laughter.

"Ah ... that guy who killed his wife?" asked Noel thoughtfully. "Why I am not surprised?"

"Selfish guy?" Martha giggled in amusement. "Why?"

"Because," said Noel. "He could love her for her kindness or her beauty or something else ... how to say? Something about her. But it was all about him. He loved her because he saw his own reflection. Like a narcissist!"

"Well, you skipped the classes, when they were teaching Shakespeare," said Jill.

"Yeah … I was in the hospital …" said Noel. "And yes, I am not well educated if that's what you mean. But I feel that Mickey is a good man."

"Invite him to Halloween," said Jill teasing, "He does not need a costume."

"That was nasty," said Noel quietly, "You didn't really mean that. Think if you were born with a huge nose and everyone laughed and bullied you for that. It wouldn't be your fault. It wouldn't be fair if people treated you this way."

"I would get plastic surgery," said Jill, feeling guilty, but still not wanting to show it.

"Yeah. Your parents can afford it. But not everyone can …" said Noel and added thoughtfully, "Plastic surgery … Do you know how much it cost?"

"Gazillions!" said Martha, "And yes, Jill, it wasn't good, what you just said. I was laughed at in school when I had acne. I tried to do whatever I could, but they were just popping up …"

"I am sorry," finally said Jill, feeling irritated with herself. "It was bad… I shouldn't…"

"I told you," said Noel, hugging her. "You didn't mean that!"

"Oh, girls!" said Martha and joined them.

Chapter 6

"Still working?" asked Mickey, when Noel opened the door of the office on a quiet knock.

"Yeah, you know ..." said Noel. She was totally ashamed of herself. Then, she took a deep breath and decided to tell the truth: "No, actually not. I've finished. But I turned on the TV, and there's a show ... I love it so much ..."

Mickey smiled. "What show?"

"*Broken*. Brian Morgan plays a therapist. Did you see it?" she said turning on the TV.

The famous face appeared on the screen, radiating intellect and charisma. Noel added, "Though this episode is not very interesting. We can go now, I guess."

Another face appeared on the screen. It was a wealthy black man about sixty, who tried to prove his point with pride and arrogance.

"What is it all about?" asked Mickey quietly.

"A therapy session, as always. The patient is a pastor. I don't quite understand the conflict; I just turned it on a minute ago."

Noel returned to her table, collecting her things into a bag and ready to go home, but Mickey slowly sat down, eyes on the screen. It looked like everything else stop existing for him. And Noel also sat down and was quietly watching more of Mickey than the show. During commercial breaks, he was totally immersed in his own thoughts, and Noel didn't want to disturb him. She was puzzled.

"I think the pastor is a totally wrong," said Noel on the way home. "He demands too much from other people and ignores his own duties. He behaves like a king, like he is totally blameless and above the law. Can you imagine him washing someone's feet?"

Mickey kept silent, and Noel continued. "I don't know, maybe in big cities, it goes this way, but our Pastor Wesley is different. He is helpful and friendly. Do you attend a church?"

"No," said Mickey with a low voice, barely audible.

"Why?" asked Noel. "Oh, I am sorry, I shouldn't! It's totally your business; I am too nosy ..."

"I was barred from ..." said Mickey and stopped abruptly.

"What?" Noel could not believe her ears. "Who could do such a thing?"

"My father," said Mickey. "He is a pastor. And he said that I couldn't go to the church. I don't deserve ..."

"How could he?" Noel was speechless.

"He wanted me to be a pastor too. My brother became a missionary. He works in Africa. Father loves him. He is very proud. But I didn't feel that I wanted to ... I quit college, and he said that he was disappointed with my decision ... That I am on a road to Hell ..." and after a silence, he added. "That I am not his son anymore."

"Oh, I am sorry," whispered Noel. "I am so sorry!"

She took Mickey's hand, and for a while, they walk in deep silence. Now Noel understood why Mickey was so mesmerized by the show.

When they reached the house, Noel suddenly stopped and faced Mickey. "You know," she said. "Sometimes people do and say things they don't really mean. About you not being his son. It was a dumb thing to say. And he'll be sorry for saying this."

Mickey just slowly shook his head and didn't say anything.

"Okay, you are right, I don't know him," said Noel. "But look, we think that older people are wiser, but they are not. I mean not all of them. They are the same children, just more pigheaded because they think they know everything."

Mickey stubbornly kept silent, looking away.

"I noticed that I became my mother's mother," said Noel. "I make decisions for her and calm her down. So can you. Grow up and be a father to him."

For some reason, Noel imagined Mickey's father exactly like that TV pastor.

"Don't listen to him; it was not his words. It was his arrogance speaking. Forgive him. You don't need to follow what he said; you need to be your own man. Without approval or permission. Just do what you want and need."

Mickey lowered his eyes and took a deep breath.

Noel felt this was a good sign. "We attend the church not because we are perfect but because we are not. Do you remember a saying about the sick people need a healer, not healthy ones?"

"Yes," Mickey said quietly and quoted by heart, "Mark 2:17. Jesus said to them, "It is not the healthy who need a doctor, but the sick. I have not come to call the righteous, but sinners.""

"Yes. We are sick; we want to be healed. To ban someone from the church is like to forbid sick people to take medicine. It is nonsense! What are we supposed to do? Lay down and die?"

Finally, Mickey raised his sad eyes to her and met her burning eyes.

She added, "I told you, it was not your father speaking. It was the spoiled kid inside him, to whom he gave too much power. But you don't give him this power over your life. Okay?"

He nodded, but still kept silent.

Laying in her bed and closing her eyes, Noel was talking to the therapist again.

"You know, Dr. Morgan, I cannot understand why people could be so cruel to each other. Especially to their own children. Why it is so hard for them just to accept us as we are? Everyone should have some people to love, some place to love, some work to love … This is so simple …"

Brian Morgan in her imagination smiled and asked, "What about your father? What would he say? Do you remember him?"

"Oh, yes," said Noel. "He was so kind and loving. He said, 'what is the point to do something you don't like? Our life becomes real torture … just follow your dreams, girl, follow your dreams'…" she thought falling asleep.

Somehow, she didn't even remember the stylish and handsome Michael Jason.

Chapter 7

———◆———

"Yes, sweetie," said Noel on the phone. "I'll make a costume for you. Would a pumpkin be okay? Oh, you want to be a princess … and Derek wants to be a pirate … I see …"

She put the receiver down and looked at Mickey, slightly rolling her eyes.

"That Halloween mess. I'll ask the girls, maybe they have some old junk …"

Days and weeks passed like a single moment. Noel had mid-term exams and could not have any distractions. After classes, she rushed to her work, and all other activity was totally out. Sometimes Mickey came and sat in the office silently reading or watching TV with the sound very low, waiting for her to finish her work.

"Trick or treat?" he asked and smiled a little.

"Sure," answered Noel. "Though I don't like to do it on the streets. We usually go to the mall. Daytime. It is better. Many people, many sweets, an ice-cream, like a formula of happiness."

"Need help?" he asked. "I don't even need a costume."

Noel blushed suddenly, recalling Jill's words. And also she suddenly realized that she even forgot about Mickey's birthmark, like it wasn't there!

She said smiling, "Yes, sure! It would be great!"

So they did. Mickey wore plastic glasses with a huge red nose attached, and Noel was in a black witch hat and robe, which she had worn every Halloween since high school. Alisha was in a slightly oversized pink princess dress, and Derek wore a pirate hat, white shirt and loose black pantaloons. They happily marched through the long brightly lit walkways of the mall covered by orange and black spiders and skeletons. The kids entered each shop meeting various sellers. Especially they liked older ladies who were giggling and totally happy.

"Oh! Who is this?" exclaimed the next Mrs. Piggy slightly hopping and waving her hands, "A pirate! Oh, I am so scared! Oh, the princess! How beautiful!"

"Trick or treat!" screeched the kids happily and received their portion of sweets.

They also collected the treats' fee from the bus passengers while the bus slowly navigated through the streets between little houses and beautiful yellow gingko and red dogwood trees and came home totally happy and sleepy.

Noel put them to bed while Tressa was entertaining Mickey with some local news and family albums. It looked like she liked him more and more. When Noel appeared from the kids' room, Tressa asked if they wanted some dinner. They refused, saying that they had eaten too many sweets that day. And suddenly Tressa said, "Maybe you wanted to walk a little? Go and have some fun. Such a warm night! Leah did."

And inde,ed it was warm despite that it was the end of October. Noel took a soft jacket and they went to a park.

There were many people wearing some scary clothes, singing and dancing in the park; some teens were trick-o-treating, some bands were playing and the people were funny and friendly. Noel lost track of time watching various performances. And when the last band left the small stage, and the huge moon was the only source of light in the park, Noel realized that it is probably time to go home. Yet, she didn't want to.

They were sitting in the first row in front of the now-empty dark stage and suddenly sounds of music appeared like a quiet wave. Someone had turned on some retro records nearby.

"*Strangers in the night*," Sinatra sang. "*Two lonely people, we were strangers in the night up to the moment when we said our first hello...*"

"So beautiful!" whispered Noel. "I love Sinatra. My dad loved him so much!"

"Want to dance?" asked Mickey.

"Oh, yes! But ... I can't! I am so clumsy!"

"Don't worry! I can help you."

"No! I cannot dance. I am so sorry."

"I really can help you. Just try?" he asked softly.

Noel nodded hesitantly. "I don't know. I don't dance…"

"No need. I'll dance for you," whispered Mickey.

"What? How?" she asked amused.

"This is how," he said, and dropped his sneakers to the ground. "Take off your shoes."

She took off her sandals and they climbed to the stage, where Mickey took her hands. "Step on my feet," and added, noticing her reluctance: "Don't worry, just do it."

She did it, and it was such an intimate touch that she held her breath. Mickey gently embraced her, and Noel put her arms to his shoulders. And Mickey made a few long strides flowing with the music. And Noel relaxed a little, also giving herself to the music and waltz-like dance.

With Sinatra's voice, she felt like a river of beautiful flying motions caught her and carried her away out of everyday life. He swayed her easily like she was weightless. She felt so comfortable in his arms, so secure; she felt like nothing bad could happen to her while she was there.

"Love was just a glance away, a warm embracing dance away," sang Sinatra, but suddenly Noel felt chilled. "No! Please stop!"

Mickey immediately stopped dancing, and she jumped from the stage to the ground and ran away to her sandals. Mickey ran after her feeling that something went wrong. He spread his arms like he wanted to comfort her but she grasped her sandals and kept them near her chest like trying to guard herself.

"Sorry," he said. "What's the matter? Did I do something bad?"

"Oh, no! Of course not! I just don't want to dance anymore."

But he still felt that something was not right. He looked at her while she was trying to look away.

Finally, she took a deep breath and realized that giving no explanation would hurt him. "Maybe it sounds dumb but … I was dreaming about dancing for many years. I asked my mom to allow me to go to a dancing class or to music school but we never had enough money and time. She was working hard, and I was babysitting my sister…" She kept silent for a while and then continued: "I felt so good dancing with you but … it was your dance, not mine. I could not even move properly. You were dancing for me … dancing instead of me! Maybe someday I'll take some classes and become your partner in dance … equal partner … so I could do it myself. I could enjoy this dance with you. Not like a burden … I feel miserable … sorry …"

And Mickey understood. His face softened; the worrying expression changed to compassion.

Sinatra's "*Too-bee-doo-bee-doo…*" sounded more and more quiet, and finally, the melody vanished. But instantly the new one started. Some amazing guitar opening played, then violins and voices; it was so tender and harmonious, so gentle. Noel really wanted to dance a slow dance. But instead, she pushed Mickey softly toward the stage and whispered:

"Could you dance for me? Just you … please?"

At that moment, the magic voice of Perry Como sounded over the beautiful music and started singing: "*I heard she sang a good song, I heard she had a style…*"

And Mickey nodded slightly, climbed to the stage, so easy like he was flying. He spread his arms, which now became like wings. His steps became again the long strides, and his entire body moved so harmoniously with the music that Noel had a spasm in her throat.

"*And there she was, this young girl, a stranger to my eyes,*" Como sang. It was so quiet and sad, so beautiful and full of pain. And Mickey was totally within this magic song, capturing the spirit of it and improvising on the spot. On this stage in the moonlight, he was now totally bonded with the music, like he had become one with it.

"*Strumming my pain with her fingers, singing my life with her words,*" Mickey was singing with his entire body. "*Killing me softly with her song...*"

"Oh, Mickey!" thought Noel, "You are killing me softly ... what are you doing in construction with this talent?"

And suddenly she understood.

When the melody finally subsided, the dancing figure slowly fell down on his knees and froze in a final gesture that looked like, "why is all this happening to me?" Suddenly, some people from the darkness started applauding and cheering, and Mickey jumped from the stage and ran to Noel, grabbed his shoes, and they dived together into the dark night.

For a long time, they walked in silence, and finally, Noel took his hand. "Are you trying to punish yourself?"

"What?" asked Mickey astonished.

"You have enormous talent! You need to be in ballet, dancing, not carrying bricks!"

Mickey kept silent, but Noel continued. "Did your father tell you that ... what happened to your girl is a punishment for your so-called 'wrong' choice of life?"

Mickey suddenly turned away. But unconsciously and convulsively he squeezed her fingers.

"Yes, he did, didn't he?" exclaimed Noel, feeling that she is right. "And you believed him!"

Mickey inhaled spasmodically, still too scared to meet her eyes.

"Mickey, it is not true! It could never be true! Can you really believe that God can kill a little girl for this?"

And because Mickey kept his silence, she continued softly: "It is not true, and I can prove it!"

When Mickey finally met her eyes, she continued quietly. "Have you ever watched some televangelists say something like: 'God thinks this' or 'God thinks that' stuff? This is so dumb! Cause no one could possibly know what God thinks! Least of all the people, who dare to talk about it so easy! Who appointed them to be God's agent? They decided it by themselves. They scare more people from the church than they attract!" She took a deep breath and kept silent for a while, calming down. Then she added softly, "God is love! And if they don't have love in their hearts, they start imagining something dumb about Him, but if you have it—you just feel it! Sometimes I watch my kids and feel so much love! And I think this is it! This is what He feels watching us. Love! When I came from the hospital with my newborn baby girl, I felt so much sadness. And I thought it is not right! This is a new life. We should feel joy! No one deserves to be met with sadness. And I talked to her, and suddenly she smiled. People say that a newborn cannot smile; it is just muscle movements. Well, maybe. But I felt it was a smile. It was like saying that everything will be okay, Mommy! And I felt love. So much love!"

She inhaled deeply and continued:

"When my kids do something wrong, what do I do? I tell them softly, what is wrong and why it is wrong. And help them not to do it again. So does He. He explains to us, what is wrong, and He is near to help when we need Him. We just need to let ourselves feel it.

"And, yes, we are just like little kids! We don't know much. We learn; we try to understand; we make mistakes. It is natural. It is normal. And someone is always here to help us to do the right things. With love."

She kept silent for a while and added softly:

"Maybe your father was not loved enough when he was a baby? He doesn't know how to do it? Have pity on him, love him, and forgive him! But do not listen to him!"

And she hugged him. Their embrace was clumsy and somewhat awkward. Mickey hugged her back gently, and Noel felt his uneven breath and soft heartbeat.

They stayed for a while, holding each other, till his breath became deep and even.

And she kissed him. Then stepped back and said softly:

"Thank you! It was a great night!"

Mickey nodded and met her eyes. His eyes were still wet but now they were bright.

Chapter 8

———— ⊶⊷ ————

"**O**h, how sweet!" said a nasty and drunk voice. "Look at them, guys! What a lovely couple!"

It was Dean, accompanied by Freddy and an unknown man; they were drunk and looked like real trouble.

Mickey pushed Noel toward her house. "Go home. Run!" Then he turned to the drunken men and said calmly, "Guys, you don't want to do that. It's time to go to sleep."

Noel, who didn't run away but stayed at a distance said, "Guys, it is really time to go to sleep! Don't make things worse!"

"Come to me, sweetie!" said Dean spreading his arms and moving toward her, but Mickey stayed in his way, watching all three approaching. He said louder, "Go home, Noel, please!"

"No, No!" shouted the men. "Come with us, baby!"

"Get out, you dirty mutant!" barked Dean and went to hit Mickey, but he jumped aside, and Dean's fist hit the air.

"Go home, guys," repeated Mickey calmly, and dived fast, as a fist whooshed through the air. He did not allow them to approach Noel, who tried to find her pepper spray and could not.

She screamed, "Fire! Fire! Help!" with all her might and tried to find something around that could be used as a weapon. The street was clean from any debris; there were no broken branches under the trees or rocks. But there were some pumpkins near the houses.

Mickey was trying to dodge the guys' fists without trying to hit back, but there were three of them. Noel saw as a couple of strikes reach Mickey's face and torso. She ran toward the house to reach a pumpkin, but Dean ran after her and grabbed Noel's elbow.

"Don't touch her!" roared Mickey. He jumped toward them and hit Dean.

The fat man fell to the ground. But the next moment Mickey himself received a strong blow to his stomach from Freddy and folded in half, as the unknown guy grabbed Noel. She didn't hesitate and kicked the guy hard, and the next moment she reached for a pumpkin with a strong hard tail and threw it with all her might to the approaching guy's face like a hammer. The guy yapped and fell down grasping his nose.

"Stop it!" roared a voice nearby. "Everybody get down to the ground!"

A man with a shotgun jumped out of his house and was now standing in the street pointing it at the fighters. "Raise your hands where I can see them!"

Everyone who was not yet on the ground, lay down, listened to the approaching police sirens.

❋   ❋   ❋

"I told you, he was defending me!" insisted Noel, explaining to the police officers. "The guys tried to grab me! Mickey didn't even want to fight!"

"Didn't want to fight?" the old cop started counting. "Couple of broken ribs, a broken nose…"

"Broken nose? It was me!" said Noel. "I hit the guy with the pumpkin. I told you, he tried to grab me!"

Mickey wanted to say something but Noel stopped him. "Don't even think to open your mouth!" and added to policemen, "We have a right to remain silent, and to make a phone call!"

"Lady," said the old cop without any attempt to conceal his irritation: "You certainly have a right to hold your tongue. No one is keeping you here. But this guy stays till we understand what happened."

"And how are you going to understand what happened if you want to kick out the only witness?" said Noel, unwavering.

"No, lady, we have four witnesses, three of them are also victims. So, it makes words of four against one!"

"Against two of us!"

"The guys say you behaved ... er ... insane." The policeman didn't even try to be polite. "Did you drink today?"

"Insane? Me?" Noel was totally shocked. "I don't drink!"

"Yeah! They said you tried to set them on fire!"

"What? They were drunk and mad!" said Noel, turning to the young policeman, who she felt was more sympathetic. "I yelled 'fire' because people in the houses would react much faster when they hear about fire than about a fight outside!"

The young cop smiled and nodded. "Well, it sounds reasonable."

And Noel added, inspired: "And I have a right to make a phone call!"

"You have all rights in the world," said the cranky policeman. "You are not under arrest. This guy is."

"No, he is not! You cannot arrest him; he didn't do anything wrong! He is a good guy. Please don't make an arrest record for him! And I need a phone!"

"Use your cell!" said the angry officer and went out of the room.

"I don't have it!" Noel said to the young cop. "Please, he really didn't do anything wrong."

"Use this one," said the young officer kindly, pointing to a phone in the office.

❅ ❅ ❅

It was after midnight, but Tressa arrived in half an hour, and she was not alone. The church minivan was packed with people; there were Pastor Wesley, a lawyer, Mrs. Lee, a journalist, a cameraman, and some more people, whom Noel didn't know. The group was impressive. The conversation was a little bit more agitated than it should be, especially when everyone tried to talk simultaneously. Tressa was the loudest.

"Yes, Frank, you are enthusiastic now," she exclaimed to the cranky policeman. "When you have an innocent boy, who tried to protect my girl from these skunks, who were fighting three against one! But where were you, when I begged you for help? Did you find my Jonah? Just to remind you, Jonah Forest, five-nine, one-eighty, brown eyes, brown hair! The last letter was from Louisiana, New Orleans. Did you forget? Eighteen years ago I filed the missing person report, so where is the result? Huh?"

Frank replied angrily: "Look, Mrs. Forest, I understand your concern—"

"No, you do not!" sharply exclaimed Tressa, "You did not raise your children alone! You are a happy family man. You don't really care about us. About anything! Every year I came to you begging about any news but you had nothing to tell me because you never even tried to find him. And did you find my son-in-law? Jimmy Strong! We asked you, but you could not care less!"

"Look, Jimmy is not missing, he probably just left for a better life."

"But he has children, who are not supported!" insisted Tressa. "Why you don't want to help? You could not care less! But this case? You are all over it! Everything is so simple. One sober guy decided to beat three drunken pigs! For what? To impress the girl? Really? Shame on you!"

"Tressa, please!" Pastor Wesley pulled her away from the police officer, "Stop it! Let Mrs. Lee do her job."

And Tressa finally obeyed. Noel also. They were sitting quietly and talking only when they were asked. Noel explained everything to Mrs. Lee, to a journalist, then to the cops, and they were left alone for a while. And finally, they all left the police department with Mickey. Everything was over.

"Let's go to a hospital," tried to press Noel, but Mickey refused.

"No hospital! Can I just go home?" he asked looking miserable.

"No!" exclaimed Noel and turned to Pastor Wesley. "He does not even have proper sanitary conditions. It is not a home. It is just a trailer near the construction site. He can't go home."

"Okay," said Pastor Wesley. "I've got the picture. I hope you don't mind if ... Mickey, will you stay in the church guest room tonight? Then we can find some place for you later. And you ladies, just go home and have a good sleep!"

And they did.

Chapter 9

———⊰⊱———

"**H**e was looking for you," said Martha playfully, when Noel came from the college. "He left a letter."

Noel opened the letter, feeling really bad.

> "*Noel, I need to go somewhere to do some important business. I'll try to be back fast. Maybe, a couple of weeks. Mickey.*"

Martha was watching Noel's face and said glumly: "Oh oh! So it happens again … I hope this time you are not pregnant." She meant it to be a joke.

"Of course not!" said Noel, trying to look normal but she didn't feel that way.

Happily, she had too little time to worry about anything except classes. But when two weeks passed, and the third one and the long Thanksgiving school break came, she was miserable. Tressa kept her morose silence. The kids were asking about Mickey, and there was nothing to tell them.

The Thanksgiving table was modest as always. They grilled a chicken instead of a turkey, had lots of apples, and a pumpkin pie, and tried to look happy. Two elderly ladies and a man from the church, who had even less than the Forest family were invited by Tressa. Their neighbor, Mr. Katz, also came and tried to cheer everyone up telling funny stories. It didn't work.

As always, Noel was mostly moving between the table, stove, and fridge, serving food to the guests. This time Leah joined her, trying to radiate optimism and telling news from her school.

When they heard the sound of a vehicle outside the house, they both looked at each other slightly scared. They both ran to the door and saw Mickey coming out of the church van followed by Pastor Wesley in a black suit and tie, holding a paper folder.

"God bless this house! Happy Thanksgiving," said the pastor, but his voice was not happy. "May we come in?"

Noel and Leah stepped aside giving them room and not understanding what is going on and what to expect.

"Would you like to share our dinner?" Noel asked.

"Thank you," said the pastor. "But let's do some business first. Can I see Tressa?"

He entered the room and was greeted by everyone.

"Mrs. Forest, Tressa, we have a word for you…"

"What?" Tressa was amused. "What word? Why do you look like you have been to a funeral? And you, Mickey, why did you disappear like that?"

"Sorry, Mrs. Forest, we have some bad news," answered Pastor Wesley. "It is about Mr. Forest. I am afraid to tell you that … you are a widow. Mickey, can you explain?"

Mickey coughed hesitantly. "Tressa, when we were at the police department, you mentioned a missing person's report…"

"Yes," she said quietly.

"Eighteen years ago," said Mickey. "Jonah Forest, five-nine, one-eighty, brown eyes, brown hair. The last letter was from Louisiana."

"New Orleans … yes, I remember."

"I took one of his pictures from your album, sorry," Mickey put a photo on the table, and Tressa took it, still slow with her reaction.

Mickey continued, "I have a friend who is a private investigator. Retired police officer. He agreed to look into it. He found him pretty fast. There was a … body of a man found not far from New Orleans with no ID and no money. Local people didn't know him; he was from some other state."

"This is his picture," said the pastor, showing the folder. "But it is not pretty. It is from the morgue."

Tressa now put her hand to her chest and closed her eyes.

"Some time later," Mickey continued. "A couple of guys were arrested with money. After interrogation, they confessed that they robbed and killed a man but they got rid of his ID and did not remember his name. They are in prison for life."

As Tressa kept silent, Pastor Wesley said, "He had found his grave too. The police didn't know, whom they could give the money to; it was about fifteen thousand. Jonah was on his way home when he was robbed."

"You said," finally Tressa managed to whisper. "You have a picture?"

Pastor Wesley gave her a folder. Tressa opened it and looked for a long time. And because the silence was so unbearable, Pastor Wesley started talking again:

"I contacted the local police and the cemetery. If you can confirm his identity, we can take him home. Our church will pay for everything and organize transportation, you don't need to worry..."

"Thank you," said Tressa, barely audible. Then she coughed and not trying to conceal her tears anymore added in a breaking voice. "It is not bad news. It was bad news eighteen years ago. But now it is good news. My Jonah is coming home." She lightly touched the image on the paper and whispered, "My darling..."

Chapter 10

"**I** am sorry for this," said Mickey, when the ceremony was over and the crowd started slowly leaving the cemetery. "I could not say about it earlier because I didn't want to give hope. And I had some business of my own too."

"Yes, I understand," said Noel quietly.

They walked in silence for a while and Mickey coughed. "I have some more bad news."

"What's this time?" asked Noel, frightened.

Mickey gave her a piece of paper, and when she unfolded it, she saw two mug shots printed. There were Jimmy and some unknown woman. Noel looked at the paper for some time and could not understand. Then slowly the meaning of the information started penetrating her mind.

It was short information from a police report about James Strong and his wife Melissa Strong, who were arrested for drug possession and selling on a school ground in a town in Mississippi. Noel looked at the pictures and text for a long time and then she crumpled the paper into a ball and threw it away.

"I hope," she said, "the kids never see him. It is better to have no father than this one." And because Mickey didn't say anything, she added, "Thank you for finding my dad. I knew it. I always knew it. That he didn't abandon us. I am so glad that Mom…" Her voice broke.

They stayed in silence for a while. Noel raised her eyes full of tears to the gray and stormy sky. It looked like the rain was coming soon.

"What are you going to do now?" she asked quietly.

"Pastor Wesley offered me a job in the church," answered Mickey, also quietly.

"What?" Noel was amused. "To do what?"

"Playing piano," said Mickey. "Part-time, temporary. Till I find something solid."

"Are you playing? Piano?" She was astonished.

Mickey nodded. "Yes, I am going to play on Sunday. Will you come?"

"Of course! I always come! The question is will you come?"

He smiled.

"I missed you," said Noel quietly and hugged him, hiding her face in his old and torn jacket and leaving some damp stains on it.

"I missed you too," whispered Mickey, and embraced her gently with so much love that she wished this moment would last forever…

Chapter 11

"*It's the most wonderful time of the year!*" Jill was singing along with the radio and hanging sparkling toys on a little pine tree in the office. The radio was transmitting endless Christmas classics, starting the first day in December.

"Yeah, the most wonderful time. Unless you are facing final exams," responded Noel, trying to read. She could not. It was cruel that she needed to study, while everyone was shopping and having the most wonderful time.

The door opened and Mr. and Mrs. Michael came to the office shaking off the winter rain from their umbrellas. In Alabama, it rarely snowed.

"Hi, Mom! Hi, Dad!" exclaimed Jill.

"Hi, girls," said Mr. Michael. "Ready to celebrate?"

"Yeah!" exclaimed Jill. "When, Dad?"

"I think we can finish totally by the twenty-third. I asked them to work even nightshifts. I will double the pay. And I'll pay holiday rates for the daytime."

"Jason," exclaimed Mrs. Michael, "Why the holiday rate? It is not a holiday yet!"

"To intensify everything, of course! And let people have some money to celebrate! The mayor is coming on the morning of the twenty-fourth. By the way, I've ordered a huge cake. Let's have a Christmas party!"

"Yeah!" Jill jumped like a cheerleader while Mrs. Michael started to make coffee.

"Er, Noel," Mr. Michael hesitated a little "Do you know Mickey quit?"

"Yes, I know," said Noel.

"Can you ask him to come back for a few days till we finish? He works really great, and I need any good worker I can get now."

"Well." Noel hesitated. "I'll ask but it is up to him."

"Yes, I know! But honestly, I believe that you have some … er … influence?"

"Yes, yes!" giggled Jill.

"Well." Noel didn't know what to tell.

"You know I was going to promote him. I mean to add him to a team. A permanent job," said Mr. Michael smiling, "He is responsible, hard-working, fast learner. This kind of ruined my plans."

Noel blushed but didn't say anything.

"Don't you want a guy with a good salary? We have a great contract!"

"What contract?" asked Jill excited.

"In Birmingham! Signed today," he exclaimed happily and waited until Jill finished her happy shrieks and jumps, while his wife laughing, covered her ears.

"I like your work too!" said Mr. Michael to Noel. "Do you want to continue with us?"

"I don't know!" said Noel even more hesitantly. "I live here, my college is here, and I don't have a car…"

"Well, it is very easy to fix," said Mr. Michael. "I can sell you mine very cheap! You have money now."

"Oh, yes?" said Noel raising her brows and looking at Jill.

The girl blushed, made a face behind her parents' back, and shook her head vigorously, mouthing silently, "No way!"

Noel smiled. Yes, they had money now. The church created a fund for the funeral and child support; some people collected money through social networks. New Orleans city promised to send a check—probably after the Pastor Wesley's intense requests—it was the money collected after the robbery that belonged to her father. What was even more amusing that Mrs. Lee had discovered that her father had life insurance, which they were assured they could collect after the holidays and all paperwork was done. Noel could buy a car now. She had just never learned how to drive it.

"We'll see." She smiled, thinking that now she could apply to the university to be a doctor, which was her longtime dream. "We'll see. My first priority now is the exam … then we'll see."

Chapter 12

$\mathcal{M}$ickey had played the piano every Sunday in the church since Thanksgiving. Wearing a new long-sleeved black T-shirt and black jeans but still unshaven and with his hairstyle unchanged, he was on the stage behind a little orchestra and played perfectly, along with other musicians.

The college church was huge and could easily accommodate more than a thousand people. There were not only students and college staff and professors but also people from the neighborhoods. Usually, the church van came to get Tressa's family. The kids loved Sundays because the children's group was full of friends, toys, and books.

It was the last Sunday before Christmas. After a great choir and concert, the pastor gave a sermon which was not long but energetic and inspiring. And then it was testimony time. One after another, young people came to the stage and told about their news. They invited people to participate in their new projects, new initiatives like to clean up the town, to restore kids' playgrounds, to collect donations to fight hunger, to create a study support group, in which successful students could help others to learn difficult subjects for free. Some people made New Year resolutions. The audience cheered and applauded. Pastor Wesley commented on each participant's speech and invited the next one.

It was like one big family, and Noel loved these moments. And from time to time she was also trying to see Mickey. But he was sitting far away with the orchestra, and she could not quite capture his expression and understand his feelings. When the pastor came to the stage again, she almost didn't pay attention to his words.

"I want to thank everyone for these inspiring speeches and great projects," said Pastor Wesley. "But I want to finish with one amazing New Year resolution one brave young lady has made. It was not actually a New Year resolution; this talk happened in the middle of the summer. But really, you don't need to wait for a New Year to start a new life, do you? It starts every moment!"

He watched the quiet congregation, full of attention and waiting for more.

"She said … well, let me first ask her permission to tell you about her decision. Noel, would you allow me to tell everyone? It would be so great if people could know about it."

Noel was totally shocked and at first she didn't understand, what he was talking about and why everyone was looking at her. Then she nodded uncertainly.

"Well, sometimes we talk," continued Pastor Wesley. "And once, this young lady told me about her wish or rather her intention to tell the truth. Always. She wanted to live her life in a way that she never tells a lie."

The quiet «wow" went through the audience, and the pastor turned to her. "Well, Noel, maybe you can come and tell us about it?"

She shook her head scared of such a huge audience but the people around cheered her and applauded, so finally she slowly rose and went to the stage.

"Well, I really don't know what to say," she said very quietly.

Pastor Wesley came and adjusted her microphone. "No worry; just tell it from your heart! What you told me."

She inhaled deeply and listening to encouraging sounds from the audience she said, "Really, there is nothing much to tell. I just thought that it is so great when people tell the truth … when you can rely on them and on what they say. I told Pastor Wesley about it. And also told that I cannot demand that from other people. All I decide is for myself.

"Well, I am not always telling the truth. Because it is simpler. And when people ask you, what are you doing now, you answer that you work … when actually you are watching TV … you just want to look good. But if I caught myself doing it, I try to tell the truth. I want to reach the goal that my every word is it. Real, truthful. That's it. I think it is good for the soul."

"What if you don't like someone?" yelled a young voice from the audience. "Should you tell about it too?"

The crowd exploded with laughter.

"I am not sure," said Noel smiling. "But I think it is not the truth. It is judgement. It is a feeling of the moment. And it could change. Some people do bad things to you, and you cannot love them right now. But it could change also. You know, it is said 'Do not judge, and you won't be judged.' That's it. Sometimes people are rough with you and you might not like them but … er … When I was in high school, I didn't like my math teacher. She was pushy and demanding, and I was angry. And now I am really sorry about it. Because now I am very good at math, recently I was offered a good job," Noel tried to look around the huge audience and spotted the familiar white head. "Mrs. Smithson, thank you so much! I love you with all my heart!"

The old woman bowed, pressing her hand to her chest with a happy smile and the audience exploded with applause. Many people stood up to see better, and finally, the teacher also stood up, happily bowing to everyone.

Pastor Wesley took a stand and said:

"Noel, thank you so much! It is a great thing you told us! And these are great words to start our prayer: Luke 6.37. Do not judge, and you will not be judged. Do not condemn, and you will not be condemned. Forgive, and you will be forgiven."

And Noel jumped back to her place in the audience, relieved and shaking from all the attention and emotions, slowly calming down for the prayer.

The pastor was saying of all the beautiful dreams of love and friendship, of all good things that could come in the future, and Noel was totally into it, dreaming that all her problems might come to the end, and maybe they finally will come to the better life.

❄ ❄ ❄

"Nice speech," said the voice behind, and it was not friendly.

Noel was standing on the church parking place watching the kids and waiting for Tressa and Leah when this voice scared her. Noel turned around and saw the old and cranky police officer, who she'd talked to in the police department on the night of the attack on her and Mickey. He was not in uniform. What was his name? Tressa called him Frank.

"Thank you," said Noel, alarmed.

"Telling the truth … it is so … good for the soul." His voice was sarcastic.

"Yes, it is good," answered Noel, even more alarmed.

"Did you ask your boyfriend about his arrest records you so worried about?" asked Frank sarcastically. "Did he tell you the truth?" And seeing Noel's total astonishment, he added, "well, I see he didn't. So ask him. If he can tell the truth."

Noel kept her silence, trying to manage her face. She couldn't. An icy chill ran along her spine.

Frank continued. "I've run him through the system. Shoplifting, illegal imports' and stolen goods' selling. Some jail time. I think you should know."

"It might be a mistake!" said Noel, feeling scared. "He has a common name!"

"Well, maybe a common name but not a common face. Such a monster! Very hard to mistake for someone else."

"Thank you," said Noel, also trying to sound ironic, "for your help."

"Serve and protect, lady. Always serve and protect," said Frank, turning to walk away.

"Well, you didn't exhaust yourself by overworking, I see," said Noel. "He found my father in three weeks. You didn't in years."

Frank gave her a glance that could not be less loving and went away.

"Don't worry," said another voice, and Noel almost jumped.

It was the young police officer from the same department. He approached, noticing their conversation and had obviously overheard some of it. He added, "Frank has been kicked out of the department, and he is not happy about it," he said apologetically. "And about your boyfriend. The problems were rather minor; the jail time was short. And nothing for the last seven years. Probably, he has been straight since then."

Noel nodded quietly to the young officer and made an attempt to smile, but in her heart, she was not comforted at all. The blood was bumping in her temples and throat;

she didn't know what to think. And she felt very lonely and losing her trust. Pastor's family, a well-educated young man, playing piano and dancing ballet … shoplifting and selling stolen stuff?

❄ ❄ ❄

Deep in the night, she was still unable to sleep.

"You know, Dr. Morgan," she was complaining in her imagination, "now, I don't know if anything he said is true … if he really is a pastor's son? What about his baby girl? He was so sincere … I want to believe him with all my heart … But did he ever tell the truth?"

She wanted to cry.

Chapter 13

───────────❈───────────

"Are you avoiding me?" asked Mickey. His voice was quiet and sad. "Did anything bad happen?"

Noel glanced at him and turned away. She was cleaning the windows of the building, the last window in the corridor on the highest floor.

"I am just tired," said Noel, looking around and seeing no one in the corridor except Mickey. "Today the results of my final exam came. I did great. Top five of the class." She put her washing stick on the floor, turned to the window, and tore some paper towels to wipe out some wet stains.

"That is great!" said Mickey, "But you look—"

"I am just tired," said Noel, but then she added, "No, that's not true—"

But Mickey also started talking simultaneously and they both stopped together.

"What?" he asked.

"No. Tell me first," she said.

"I …" he started hesitantly. "I wanted to tell you … no … later … first, I want to tell you that I love you! I want you to know that. You and Lisa are the best that happened in my life. Ever!"

Noel blinked under his intense stare. Her lips were trembling.

"I love you," he continued. "You've changed my life, and it was like a miracle. I want to ask you to marry me but before that … I need to tell you something."

He was nervous and started breathing deeply and finally managed to continue. "May I ask you? Well, sorry, I am a total mess now." He glanced down from the window and seeing some attention from below took Noel's hand and led her away from the window.

"I know I cannot ask you before I tell you the total truth. I was married, and I left also to finalize some paperwork. Now I am a free man, you know. It is over. But it is not important … Well, it is. But it is not, what I wanted to tell you." His eyes were now intense and burning from inside.

"If it's about your arrest records … I know about it," said Noel finally. "Frank told me."

"What?" The total amusement on his face was so genuine that Noel was confused again.

"Your records. Shoplifting … selling illegal … er …"

"Oh." His reaction was somewhat different from what she expected. "That…" He looked like he recalled something totally unexpected and not important at all. He suddenly spoke passionately: "I can explain! I'll explain everything. I ask only one thing. Don't reject me instantly. Okay? Please, don't say 'no' at once. Give me time."

"Well…" said Noel hesitantly and suddenly scared.

"Promise? Please! Promise me!" He was begging.

"Well, what exactly? Not saying 'no' if I want to?"

"Yes, just postpone it. Please!"

"Well … okay, I promise. But please finally tell me—"

"Yes! Thank you! It is great!" He gasped for air, and then inhaled deeply a few times. "Remember, back in the church, you told that you decided to tell the truth … it was so great! It was amazing! And I want to do it too but … what if…"

He paused again.

"Imagine you have a dream. Not a daydream but like … you fall asleep and see a beautiful life, no troubles, no grief. Everything is great; people you love, your friends, and your family surround you … you are so happy."

Noel had a feeling that he was talking about his daughter. He sees her alive and well.

"Like Heaven. Yes, I understand," she whispered.

"And maybe you even know this is not true. You know it's a fairytale, and the moment will come when you wake up and see the reality. But you don't want to. Because at that moment you lose your dream! You want to keep it just a little bit more … just a moment or two." He stopped hesitantly.

Noel didn't know what to say, and he continued passionately, "Then you wake up, and everything is different, and the happiness is gone."

"Well," she smiled, "I never had such dreams because I never had time for it. Life comes to me shaking and yelling 'Mommy, wake up, I want a strudel'—"

She stopped because she realized that her reality actually *is* his dream ... she cursed herself for the last remark; it was a cruel thing to say to the man, who cannot have such awakenings.

"I am sorry," she said quietly. "I think I understand what do you mean. The problem is ... what if your happiness is on the way in reality too? What if you just need to face it? You can't meet it until you wake up."

He stared at her with a deep question in his eyes.

Finally, he also inhaled. "Yes, You're right. You're right... I can't find it until—"

"Noel!" yelled Jill from the staircase door. "Mickey! Did you finish there? Can you help?"

For the next few hours, they didn't have a chance to talk. When it was almost midnight, Mr. Michael, Martha, and some other people with cars delivered everyone to their houses, and Noel didn't have a minute to think about anything; she fell asleep the moment her head touched the pillow.

Chapter 14

———— ❈ ————

"**M**ommy, look!" Derek was shaking her vigorously.

"What sweetie?" Noel opened her eyes with difficulty. She'd certainly had no time to dream.

"Look!" Derek pulled her toward the window, where Alisha was standing and watching too.

It was December 24th, early morning, and the sunrise was yet to come but there was no darkness anymore. White puffy snowflakes were slowly gliding to the ground, covering everything with a furry carpet. It was so beautiful!

Wrapping herself with a blanket over her pajamas, Noel opened the door and the kids rushed outside. It was the first snow in her children's lives.

"*I'm dreaming of a white Christmas…*" someone was singing in a beautiful voice in the street.

"Happy birthday, young lady!" said Mr. Katz. He was standing in his door frame too. "How's the divine gift?"

"What gift?" Noel asked, smiling and spreading her palms to catch some snowflakes.

"This gift!" answered Mr. Katz, also spreading his arms. "Don't you see? It didn't snow in years! This is a kind of a miracle! Good sign."

"Merry Christmas," said Noel, feeling unexpectedly happy.

"And happy Hanukkah to you too!" said the neighbor with a deep bow. "God loves this time for miracles! Magic time! Don't you think?"

❄ ❄ ❄

"He has a ri-i-i-ng!" teasingly sang Jill, when Noel entered the office.

"What? Who?" asked Noel.

"Who? You are asking, who?" Jill rolled her eyes. "I saw him nearby, opening a little box… Oh! They are coming! They are coming!" and she jumped out of the trailer.

Noel hesitantly left the office. A crowd was forming a circle around the little stage. People were mostly gathering close to the action, but Noel stayed near the entrance to the square and close to the office.

The building was totally transformed to a shining beauty. Christmas decorations covered some lower floors' windows; the red velvet band was stretched symbolically in front of the entrance. A beautiful Christmas tree sparkling with glittering balls and real snow, had been erected on the left side of the entrance. The square was full of elegant ladies and men in suits and coats. There were also reporters and cameramen. Some expensive cars delivered some important guests, the mayor, and the staff. A small military orchestra was playing cheerful Christmas classics under a canopy.

Noel didn't listen much; she was just enjoying the snowfall. It was weakening now but still good enough to create holiday joy, even with the low cloudy sky.

She spotted Mickey far away in the opposite part of the crowd circle. He was easy to spot because of his messy hair and dark red bandana; he was helping other workers to make some last moment fixes. They didn't have a chance to finish their talk yesterday; Noel had left about midnight when he was still installing and decorating the Christmas tree somewhere high above.

"Today is the day," she thought suddenly, "when, finally, he tells everything … or I don't know, what I am gonna do!"

The program started, but she could not pay attention to what the mayor and other guests were saying. And she also thought, what if he really wants to come with this ring in front of all these guests … oh, she hated these scenes! This is why she stayed as close to the office as possible to escape when … if … well … never mind. Just to escape.

But what no one expected was the appearance of an enormous black limousine just at the moment when Mr. Michael, the mayor and some other important representatives came to cut the red band. They paused for the cameras; but when they actually cut the band, the cameras were turned to that limo, which carelessly parked diagonally on the road totally blocking the exit from the square.

The orchestra made some strange noises and the music died; the amused crowd was silently watching the people coming out of the limo. And because Noel was the closest to these new guests, she was the first to be shocked.

The first person out of the car was Brian Morgan. The Dr. Morgan of her night conversations, the TV star, which poster she had on the wall over her table! The next person was a man, whose name Noel didn't remember. He was blond and also Hollywood famous, but Noel could not see anyone except the celebrity of her dreams. Well, the second celebrity of her dreams.

"It looks like they are partying or something," said Morgan to another man and turned around to find someone. He met Noel's eyes. "What is this all about? Christmas party? Doesn't look like it."

"Who cares?" answered the Hollywood star uncaringly. He started shaking snowflakes from his multi-thousand-dollar suit, offended. "Who ordered that?"

"The building ..." said Noel to Brian Morgan and choked. "O ... Opening..."

Morgan smiled at her kindly and said to the blond, "Well, Garry, I think we have to wait."

"No way I'll wait under this stuff."

"I think we should. Don't break their celebration!"

"Well, dear Brian, in this middle of nowhere I think we *are* the best part of their celebration," and he also turned to Noel. "Right?"

She gulped.

Morgan smiled and repeated, "We should wait."

"Well, stop me if you can!" said Garry arrogantly and went to the middle of the circle spreading his arms, looking around, and yelling: "Well, hello, hello, hello! Ho-ho-ho! I am almost your Santa Claus! Merry Christmas! Baby, where are you? Go daddy!"

"Where is he?" asked Morgan to another man from the limo, and Noel almost choked again.

He was … was he? Well, no, he wasn't. But the first moment she had the impression that he was the first celebrity of her dreams, the television star, Michael Jason. He looked so much like him, the same neatly cropped hairstyle, the same elegant clothes. But by the second moment, Noel saw some difference. He looked more like Jason's brother.

"That one." Jason's brother, pointed to someone far away.

That man was wearing dark red bandana and familiar denim jacket. And he was slowly coming out of the crowd to the middle of the circle toward the limo and the guests. Toward Noel.

"Ho-ho-ho!" exclaimed Garry spreading his arms. "Hello, baby! Merry Chris—wow! What happened to your face?"

But Mickey passed him without paying any attention. He was looking only at Noel, as the celebrities and all the people around were not important at all. Their eyes locked. Noel thought she might faint; she could not comprehend what's going on.

Mickey took his bandana off his head and made some gesture like wiping his mouth with it or spitting something into it. And suddenly his protruding jaws became … well … not protruding anymore. The shape of his face had changed. He was coming closer, and Noel already recognized deep despair in his eyes, focused on her. Then he touched his forehead and suddenly peeled his dark swollen birthmark away from his face. People in the crowd made a short screech, but there was no blood. It was just a clear dark skin on his smooth and handsome face. Very handsome face.

After a moment of silence, a piercing scream exploded in the air. Martha, Jill, and some other women in the crowd were pressing their palms to their cheeks and screaming with all their might. Because the man was now recognizable.

Noel gasped. This was too much.

He *was* Michael Jason in the flesh.

Not that elegant and clean shaven like in the movie, with messy hair and untrimmed stubble but it was undoubtedly him. He was approaching slowly under the numerous cameras and streaming cell phones, looking at Noel and she could not bear it anymore. She turned away and ran to her office as fast as she could.

He was faster. And when she rushed through the door, he was also after her inside, instantly closing and bolting the door.

"Please, please, please!" he was whispering in her ear, hugging her gently. "Please let me explain!" Please! You promised to give me some time!"

She was shaking all over and could not say anything.

"Please, you promised," he was begging her.

"Was it a joke?" Finally she screamed. "Are you playing with me?" She suddenly started crying. "Why? Why? You were lying to me!"

"Noel, dear, my darling!" he was calling her with all the loving names he could now, "Please! I love you with all my heart! But you see, the moment the truth came out – the dream disappeared. Please give me a chance! Few weeks, few days! It is still me! If you loved me ugly, maybe you can love me when I am not—"

She was still crying: "You played with me! It was all a lie!"

He was saying softly and lovingly, "It was not a lie! I just wanted to disappear from my life! I wanted to live without cameras. It was an illusion, yes, and a dream! Like I am no one and nobody. A man from a crowd, that's all! I was in despair after what happened to Lisa. It is all true. And I have a friend, Mickey, Michael Birch; I've known him since elementary school. He is from a very poor family, and he is my best friend. He was the only one who came to me, when … who really cared about me, who was really sorry … he had this birthmark for real. And he once complained about how people treated him badly. And suddenly I had this thought … what if? I helped him to get plastic surgery to remove the mole.

I asked him to swap our IDs for a while. I asked him to help me to disappear to have some time to think.

"And I was sitting on a bus, which drove me through the middle of nowhere, a new man with a new face, which scared everyone. And it was good. It was so good! Everyone wants to look away. No one cares. Just no one! The first time in many years I felt free. I felt I wanted to live, to understand why all this is happening to me. What to do now with my life? And I prayed about … If there is any hope for me, oh, Lord, please, give me a sign … And in one of the towns, I saw the banner on the building under construction 'Jason Michael and Co.' Just like my name turned around, Michael Jason. And I thought that's it! And I came to work here. And I met you."

She was not shaking anymore but she was still not feeling good. It was really too much. She felt like her heart was frozen. She kept silent.

He was softly comforting her, patting her face, her hair and talking, begging. "All I want is just a chance! Just don't say 'no' right now. Give me some time. You promised."

"Okay," she managed to say quietly. She inhaled deeply and added with her eyes down, "Okay … I am too tired now … I just want to tell … I cannot say to you 'I love you' if I don't feel it. You know."

"I know."

"And I don't feel anything now except … I am scared … and torn … and confused."

"Just don't say no," he begged again. "Be my friend for a while? Please?"

She could not say anything, just nodded a little. He gently embraced her, kissing her hair and whispered. "Thank you."

That moment, the crowd outside the trailer exploded with long and rejoicing "Yeah!" Because every little crack in the window blinds was now a way to see the best reality show ever.

"Well," said Michael Jason. "That's what I worried about."

"I want to go home," said Noel, scared and almost crying again.

"Let's go," he said, and they did.

The trip crumbled into chaos in Noel's mind. People with their cameras and cellphones, shrieks and questions, the long and quiet limo, where Mickey, well, now Michael, felt himself pretty much at home discussing some issues with others, the issues, which Noel could not comprehend and barely could hear. And all that attention from these celebrities! She felt as if she was under the microscope, all naked and defenseless.

She was totally relieved when they finally reached their destination. No need to explain anything to the family because now they had television and watched the building opening unfold in all details. Leah opened the door, and she was very excited. She now also had a cellphone and was happily streaming the video. Noel snapped at her and stopped this madness.

"What happened to your face?" asked Derek.

He was hugging his alligator and watching the guests entering. For some strange reason, he didn't have any trouble immediately recognizing his friend Mickey.

Michael Jason squatted down to have their eyes on the same level and smiled with a sad smile.

"Your mom kissed me, and the spell disappeared."

"And you became Prince Charming?" asked Derek, touching Michael's nose and cheek, where the birthmark was before.

"Well … sort of…" said Michael uneasily, and looked at the smiling guests.

Chapter 15

"*I* don't understand why can't you answer me?" said Garry to Michael Jason with irritation in his voice. "I was looking for you! I need the answer as soon as possible! This is why I am here! There are millions on hold!"

Michael shrugged like the millions were not important at all. He turned to Noel and explained.

"He wants me to be in a movie, which I don't like."

"If you don't like it, then don't do it!" said Noel quietly. "What is the point to do something you don't like?"

"Dear girl, you don't know what you are talking about!" Snapped Garry. "There are millions—"

"I am not your dear girl, Mister What's-your-name," said Noel calmly. "And we have money!"

"She said what's-my-name?" The astonished guest turned to Michael. "I am Garry Fervent, who has a star in the Hollywood Walk of Fame, who played in tens of movies and who has a film production company … and she said what's-my-name? She is lying! Right?"

"She does not," answered Michael. "She never lies."

❄ ❄ ❄

The rest of the day for Noel consisted of unconnected episodes. The Hollywood guests in her dining room were somewhat ridiculously mixed with her elderly poor neighbors, invited by Tressa. The happiest person around was Leah, who took selfies with every guest. The next happiest was Mickey Birch, the man who looked like Michael Jason's brother. His jaws were naturally protruding forward; some tiny scars were visible on his face.

"You have no idea," he said with a strong street accent and happy smile, "Out of what they cut my skin! You really don't want to know!" They laughed with Leah. He was the only one of the guests who felt very natural amongst the elderly neighbors and who had no trouble saying a prayer before the meal; the other guests were just trying to indulge.

❄ ❄ ❄

"Why can't we go now?" insisted Garry Fervent. "A few days of vacation, it's a great time to decide! Right now!"

"I cannot go," said Michael Jason. "This afternoon at three I am playing piano in the church. I promised. It is Christmas Eve, you know."

"In the church? You are playing in the church?" He was totally astonished.

"Why not?" asked Brian Morgan, turning to Noel. "I started singing in church. It was a great part of my life."

"But then we can go? Right?" asked Garry, this time turning to Noel like finally accepting that she was real and important.

"I'll think about it," she said quietly.

"Oh my goodness! A few days of vacation in Hollywood! It is beautiful! I'll even say a magic word! Please?"

❄ ❄ ❄

It was the most unusual Christmas Eve celebration in the church. The entire town was there—from the mayor to construction workers. Pastor Wesley was overwhelmed by emotions. Sometimes, he forgot the words of the sermon, but no one blamed him because no one could keep calm in this situation. Michael Jason was playing piano, and Brian Morgan was singing. His deep velvet voice was so beautiful! He sang "Silent Night," and "Mary, Did You Know?" and some other lovely songs. And everyone was totally happy.

Except for Noel. She was probably the only person in the entire church who was not excited and moved. She felt frozen.

❄ ❄ ❄

"Well, baby, don't you worry," said Tressa calmly after the sermon. "Pastor Wesley just invited me and Leah to celebrate Christmas with his family tonight. I think we'll go."

"No!" shrieked Leah. "I can go with them and help with the kids!"

"No, darling! You go with me and let them be alone," said Tressa, calming her down. "They need it."

❄ ❄ ❄

It had been a really, really long day! At the end of it, Noel found herself on the huge, luxurious and almost empty private airplane. She didn't want to talk with anyone and requested that they all leave her alone with the kids. The children, who ran around the airplane about a thousand times, were now happily asleep in comfortable armchairs, transformed to safe and soft beds. A nice flight attendant appeared noiselessly from time to time, ready to fulfill her every wish. But Noel could not sleep. She was thinking and could not come up with any idea of what to do.

Unexpectedly, she felt a very soft touch on her shoulder. Brian Morgan was standing near her chair, asking her with a courteous gesture to come with him. She looked at her kids and nodded.

When she followed Morgan to his compartment, she saw Michael Jason, who was sitting on the other side of the aisle near the oval window pretending to be asleep. She passed by trembling, feeling uneasy.

Brian entered his compartment and invited Noel to the chair in front of him. His smile was kind and soft.

That smile, those eyes she watched enchanted so many times on the television. And now it was for her for real.

"Do you want a drink?" he asked softly.

"I don't know," she said.

"Well, then let me offer you some tea?"

She nodded, barely understanding what he was talking about and almost didn't notice the beautiful porcelain cups that appeared on the table with a fresh aromatic bakery.

"You have such a sweet home," he said gently and even dreamy. "Loving home. It is such a treasure!"

"Yes," she whispered.

"I had a pretty hard life for some years. For many years, actually. When I was not famous. I always wanted to have such a loving and sweet home. Never succeeded. Rich home? No problem. Loving home? Never." He sighed. "How are you doing? Is it hard? Michael said you want to be a doctor?"

Noel nodded, shrugged, smiled a little, opened her mouth, and could not say anything.

"Don't worry. You don't need to tell me if you don't want to. I am sorry; I didn't want to be intrusive … Take some bread; it is fresh and delicious."

"Thank you," finally managed Noel. "Thank you, Dr. Morgan…"

"I am not a doctor, you know," he smiled.

"Oh, yes …" Noel blushed, smiled a little, and lowered her eyes. She sipped some tea and added: "Yes … We are okay … just … yes, it is hard…"

She sighed and unexpectedly started talking. She was really talking to these amazing and bottomless eyes full of attention and love … For real! Not a fantasy! And she discovered herself unloading on him her life, her dreams, and her hopes. And how she felt about Mickey, and what she feels now, when … she stopped.

"When now he is a different man?" asked Brian.

"Yes!" she said quiet and sad. "You know I love him so much! But I love Mickey! My Mickey! Not this man! And thinking that he does not exist anymore… never existed… makes me feel…" She started crying quietly and took the tissue he offered. "He said he is the same. I understand it in my mind, but I don't feel it! I can't! Everyone around is happy for me! I think I should be happy too, but I am like frozen inside!"

Then she stopped abruptly and asked him with an embarrassed smile through tears. "How many times do people start talking to you like you are a real therapist?"

"All the time," he smiled sympathetically, "It happens all the time. And this is a great privilege. People share with me their lives, what's in their hearts. I treasure these moments."

They kept silent for a while, listening to the soft humming of the powerful airplane, then Morgan sipped some tea and accurately placed the cup back to the plate. He sighed and looked in Noel's eyes again.

"You know," he said, "I am not a therapist. I can't give you a professional advice. But maybe you can accept a friendly one?" After a pause, he had her full attention. "You know, there are carnivals, where people wear masks. And when they do it, they feel enormous freedom. They drink, they fight, they vandalize, they have wild sex, they do many bad things because they feel free from all the limitations that society puts on them. They think they hide themselves with the masks, but actually, they opened their real souls. They showed who and what they truly are."

He paused and then continued softly. "So, Michael wore a mask, and what was he doing then?"

Noel waited for him to continue, but he added with a smile, "Don't expect it from me; I wasn't there. You were. So, what was he doing?"

Noel shrugged, looked down and slowly said: "Nothing … well … working … working hard. Reading, helping us, fixing the house, giving us money … playing piano in the church."

"Well … not bad after all," said Brian smiling.

"He found my father," said Noel softly. "His grave."

That sat in silence for a while, then Morgan continued again. "You may say you saw his real soul. And you loved him even through his strange appearance."

They kept silence for a while.

"It is still," Noel said quietly, "it is different. I thought he was poor."

"Actually, he is. When all this happened with his daughter … Well, first I need to tell you he fell in love with a woman, who loved only money. And the worst thing is that I feel responsible.

"I made him famous. He was just an assistant working with light, electricity, and all this stuff. But he was so good looking that I gave him an episode, and he did great! Next, I gave him a real role and he became a star instantly. In one of the movies, I invited her. Did you see any Hollywood news about them?"

"No."

"Good! Don't watch it; it was nasty. They got married, and in two years their marriage fell apart; she sucked lots of money out of him and took the girl accusing … well … don't watch it, it is all lies. I know them both so well. Then the horrible accident happened." Morgan was silent for a while and then continued sorrowfully. "I was far away. When I came home, people told me that he donated everything he had to some children's hospitals and to the charitable fund made in the name of Lisa. He just gave everything away and disappeared. People said he was in a sort of rehab or retreat in Europe or maybe even Japan. No one knew. But his credit cards were never used, and his bank accounts are empty. So now he really has nothing. If he'll make the contract, it will be another story. But right now …"

"Is his father really a pastor?" asked Noel.

"Yes. I tried to communicate with his family and understood why he … why they didn't know where he is."

Suddenly Noel realized something: "Does he look like … that pastor in your show, *Broken*, in which you played a therapist and one of the patients was a pastor?"

Morgan smiled. "Oh, yes, it was him. Mickey disappeared, and I wanted to send him a message. I hoped that he might see one of these episodes—"

"Well, he did," said Noel.

Morgan smiled and nodded a little. "I am glad he got the message. It is not a popular show. I did a lot to push it to this channel. Hoping. Well … I am glad I succeeded."

"It is not true," exclaimed Noel. "That it is not popular. I love it! It is the best show ever! It makes me think and understand people better. It is so great."

"Thank you! When I make the next episodes, I'll be thinking of you. But yet, it is not the most popular show financially. Not so many people watch it—"

Suddenly something started beeping quietly.

Morgan looked at his watch and smiled. "Well," he said, "I need to leave you for a few minutes. I have some important things to do."

And he left to go to the tail of the airplane.

Noel sat in silence and deep in her thoughts. It was like all her last days passed by in front of her eyes. Something strange was happening in her mind and soul. It was like a huge chunk of ice inside started melting. She remembered his dance in the park, his playing in the church, his words, his voice, when he said, "I had a baby." She just tried to see him with a different face.

Tears came to her eyes. She stood up and slowly went back to her kids. And when she reached Michael's chair, she saw his shoulder and his palm with the picture of Lisa. And the last piece of ice in her heart finally disappeared. It was like a sudden recognition. It was like two images finally became one.

Mickey put the photo of the girl on his knee and covered it with his palm again. He was looking into a dark window. Noel sat quietly on the next chair feeling so much compassion for him that her chest could not bear it anymore. She put her palm on his and whispered, "Mickey …"

It was though a slight electric charge went through their arms. He turned to her, blinked few times like he was scared or could not believe his eyes. Finally, he took a deep and sporadic inhale like he could not breathe for a long, long time and finally reached the air.

"Mickey," she whispered. "I missed you so much!"

She too inhaled deeply, seeing how his facial expression changed from deep despair to hope. No, she could not see his face; she could see only his eyes. They were real; they belonged to her Mickey. Her feelings were coming back like a sun rising slowly in her heart. She took a deep breath. "Just don't lie to me. You know, it was like falling into an abyss. I mean, when you lose your trust it is like losing the ground. Everything is falling down. I might not survive one more time."

He touched her cheek gently and whispered, "It will never happen. I promise."

He looked into her eyes for a long time, then pulled her gently to him and held her close. She put her head to his shoulder and had this feeling like when they were dancing in the park. That feeling that nothing bad could happen to her when she is in his arms.

"I love you," he whispered into her ear.

"I love you too," she whispered back, feeling it with all her heart.

They forget about time.

Suddenly a melodious tinkle woke them up to reality.

"Ho-ho-ho!" said someone nearby quietly. "Merry Christmas!"

Brian Morgan, came from the tail of the airplane wearing Santa's red and white outfit and a gorgeous white beard carrying two glasses of champagne. "Merry Christmas, kids!" He offered the glasses of sparkling drink to Noel and Michael.

People were gathering together. Passengers, flight attendants and the crew in uniforms were taking champagne glasses from the little table. Derek and Alisha also came; they were blinking sleepily and happily at Santa.

"Merry Christmas!" said Santa softly.

"Merry, Merry Christmas!" People were saying to each other with happy smiles as they clinked each other's champagne glasses.

"*Noel, Noel, the angels did say!*" Morgan sang in his beautiful velvet voice.

"It's Christmas already … Yesterday, Christmas Eve, was my birthday," Noel whispered to Mickey.

"Oh, my!" said Michael, "Really? Sorry, I didn't know about it! I don't even have a gift!"

"You already gave it to me. And by the way, you have a ring. Jill told me she saw it." Noel smiled.

"Well." His smile was embarrassed. "It is too cheap. Not even a diamond…"

"It is not cheap," said Noel. "If it is from your heart, it is the best gift ever."

He smiled, got down on one knee and took a little box from his pocket.

Garry Fervent sipped some champagne and slightly punched Santa with his elbow. He whispered thoughtfully, "About a marriage made in heaven … a bit too literally, don't you think? You cannot show it in the movie; it is too much of a cliché."

They smiled at each other, and Santa answered:

"Well, tell me, what isn't a cliché?"

Garry raised his brows, finished his champagne and whispered with enthusiasm. "Wow! You're right! You are so right. You know, Santa, about those millions on hold … I think we can drop this idea. Jason doesn't like it anyway. I have another wish for you. I think we can come up with another story, which is much, much better. Right?"

Santa shook his head and chuckled quietly. Some things never change in the world!

"*Noel, Noel, the angels did say*!" The music played somewhere. The airplane was carrying them far away with all their hopes and dreams about a better life, and a huge headlight beam was powerfully shining through the night clouds.

And who knows? Maybe some of the hopes and dreams could eventually come to life.

It was Christmas after all.

Acknowledgements

I would like to express my deep gratitude to my dear friends Laura Gore, Peggy Rooney, and Annie Seaton for great help with writing and editing the story.

My grateful thanks are also extended to the Healing Hope support group in the Grace Baptist Church in Bowie, Maryland.

I would like to extend my thanks to the people of Alabama A&M University and Oakwood University Church in Huntsville, Alabama.

My deepest love and appreciation to my dear husband and loving sons.

And finally, I especially wish to thank the unknown neighbor with the huge birthmark on his face for the very idea of the story.

❄ ❄ ❄

Printed in the United States
by Baker & Taylor Publisher Services